GOAT TALES

AuthorHouse™
1663 Liberty Drive
Bloomington, IN 47403
www.authorhouse.com
Phone: 1 (800) 839-8640

This book is printed on acid-free paper.

ISBN: 978-1-7283-6344-8 (sc)
ISBN: 978-1-7283-6345-5 (e)

Library of Congress Control Number: 2020910016

Print information available on the last page.

Published by AuthorHouse 06/01/2020

authorHOUSE®

GOAT TALES

ROSE CASTLEBERRY

I dedicate this book to my daughters
Seather and Hara
I mean Heather and Sarah
They are the brightest starts
In my universe,

Goat Tales

INTRODUCTION: Goat Tales are a series of adventures told by the farm's goat, Gretta. The tales are about the lives of the animals on the farm and their adventures. Many of the things they experience are not much different from our children's lives. Gretta is full of tales. The tales are about different life learning adventures that are experienced by the animals on the farm. The reader will also benefit from these adventures in navigating youth and preparing them for life and developing social skills. Hay! Here comes Gretta now.

Hello! My name is Gretta the Goat, but you can call me G.G. I live on a farm that is owned by a man named Mr. Charmer, we call him Farmer Charmer. You know farm life is a lot of work. But, you would not guess what happens in the lives of the animals on the farm. You would not believe it! A lot of things happen, like when Charlie a sea gull was found in the chicken coop with the chickens. We had a swoosh monster, and everyone was afraid to go outside. Because every time they heard "swoosh" someone disappeared. One day there was an egg found on Farmer Charmers doorstep and no one knew how it got there. One time Clatter the goose found magic sticks she could ride. One fall we had a pumpkin explosion! That is just a few of the things that has happened. The stories are all something I like to call my goat tales because I am a goat and I like to tell them, and I am the keeper of all the stories. I consider myself the farm historian.

I am getting so excited to tell you about my stories that I am getting ahead of myself. Each animal is unique, and I mean unique, I cannot wait to tell you about all of them and their adventures. You may think that their life is very much different from yours, but in some ways it is not.

I should start at the beginning. Let me think, what story shall I begin with? Oh, I know! I should begin with Penelopy Hen and Johnny her adopted chick and how Johnny becoming our rooster. But wait! First, I need to tell you a little bit about the farm. You know, describe it so you can picture it.

The Farm

On the farm we have a pond which is enjoyed by all. There is a big red bard and Farmer Charmer lives in a white wood house with a big front porch with a swing. He has a white picket fence on all four sides of the house to keep the animals out, especially me. Seams we tear up the lawn and eat all the garden but I must say Pearl the pig does her share of the crime. The front gate has flowers growing on it.

There are fields of corn and hay growing in all directions around the farm. There's all kinds of animals, horses, cows, pigs, goats, geese, and chickens.

A lot of the stories have something to do with Johnny as our rooster. Johnny had a lot to overcome before he became our rooster. But I think all that made him a better rooster. You see, it all started like this...

One day an egg was fond laying on Farmer Charmers door.

"What is this?" He said. "An egg left in front of my door?!"

He did not know why it was there or how it got there but that was not important right now. He had to get the egg taken care of properly fast or it would not hatch. The egg was still warm. So, he had a little time left before it was too late. He had to find a hen to set on it and keep it warm, and he had to find a hen fast. "I have to find out who it belongs to". He asked all his hens, but no one claimed it. Each hen said she did not lay it. They told him they had all the eggs they could take care of. He had to do something quick because the egg had to be properly taken care of right away.

"I know what I will do" he said. "I will see if Penelopy Hen would like to have it"!

You see, Penelopy Hen was a nice hen who had never been able to lay eggs. Because she had never laid an egg, she did not have any chicks. All the other chickens had chicks and that made her feel bad. She wanted to raise chicks too. The chickens would say things to Penelopy that was hurtful to her. Worst of all, the other hens gave Penelopy a hard time because she did not have chicks. They would say it was only teasing. If you ask me if the teasing hurts, then it is bulling and that is bad! Penelopy wanted to have chicks so bad, she knew she would be a good mother hen. She prayed for a miracle so she could have a family. When Farmer Charmer asked Penelopy if she wanted the egg to have as her own, she said: "Yes! Yes!" Penelopy was so happy! She was happy to get the egg. Her miracle had happened, her prayer was answered. It was only one egg but still a blessing. Penelopy was going to have a family!

Penelopy did take good care of the egg. One day it hatched and out came the ugliest chick you have ever seen. The chick had big feet and long legs. In fact, it was taller than all the other chicks because its legs were so long. That chick could barely operate them because they were very wobbly. Its neck was too long as well, everyone wondered how its long neck could hold up that big head. The chick had a face that they said only a mother could love, and she did. To Penelopy it was beautiful, and awkward but unique. She named it Johnny, simply because she liked that name and depending on the spelling it would work for a male or female. You see when chicks are first born you cannot tell if they are male or female. She was sure this chick was going to mature into a rooster. You see, a chick is about 4 weeks old when it starts to show if it is going to be male or female. Penelopy could not have loved it more if she had laid the egg herself, and Farmer Charmer loved that chick as much as he did all of his chickens. Even though he did not know where it came from.

Farmer Charmer said "that chick definitely did not look like all the rest of his chickens".

All the chickens really said hurtful things to Penelopy and Johnny when he was growing up because he did not fit in. Even the rooster picked on him when he should have been protecting Johnny from the bullies. I guess you could say he was a bully too. The chickens teased him because his feathers were different and not the same color as theirs. I wish I had time to tell you more about what happened to Johnny and the other animals on the farm. Johnny grows up with many challenges to face and fears to overcome. He becomes a young rooster that is very insecure. Because of the Swoosh Monster he grew up afraid to leave his mother's side. He also had to overcome all the negative things said to him and about him. The chickens that teased him were going to become under his care in the future. Basically, you could say he became the boss over them. Is he going to forgive them for the things they said, or get even? The rooster has a lot of responsibilities, the safety of everyone in the chicken coop for one and he makes the rules. I will tell you, the first rule Johnny made when he became the rooster was that no one could tease or pick on anyone else. He remembered how it felt and vowed to not allow any type of bullying anymore. I cannot tell you all about the journey that Johnny takes from chick to rooster now because I see Farmer Charmer left his gate open again and took the tractor to the fields. So, that means I have a garden to protect. Pearl the pig will be in there eating and uprooting everything in sight! Oh! Oh! After I protect the garden maybe I can stand on top of his car while he is gone. I love it up there! He hates it when I do that. Got to Go! Come back soon, for another story about the animals on Farmer Charmers farm. Oh, and I have got to tell you about the Swoosh Monster.

Later That Day

I'm back!

G.G. here.

Pearl the pig beat me to the gate and Mrs. Charmer herded Pearl away with her broom. So, there were no garden treats for her today. Mrs. Charmer also used the broom on me when I got near the car. So back to my tale. Where did I get to? I was about to tell you the Tale of how Johnny became the rooster in charge of us all!

Life in the Chicken Coop

There was not much to do in the chicken coop. There was scratching and pecking at the ground to get seeds and digging up worms. Chasing the occasional bug that wondered into the chicken yard was great fun. But the chick's favorite thing to do was to play chase. Sometimes all the chicks would join in and it would be great fun. All this while they tried to stay out of trouble with Bruster the Rooster.

Bruster is the farms only rooster. Bruster controlled everything that went on in the chicken coop and the chickenyard. None of the chicks wanted him to have a reason to scold them. He could be mean when he did. Bruster had been the rooster for the farm for a long time. Sometimes, some of the chicks would have an argument over who found the bug or grain first and Bruster would have to break up the fight. Usually he did that by eating it himself.

Penelopy Hen always kept a close eye on Johnny to make sure her chick was staying out of trouble and safe. The other chicks were sometimes mean to Johnny by teasing Johnny about being so tall, or having big feet, some would even tell him he was ugly. Penelopy told Johnny that he needed to pay them no attention and hold his head up. Someday he would be a beautiful bird and they would wish they had not treated him the way they did. Johnny asked Penelopy why he was different, he looked different and felt different. She would tell Johnny what a blessing he was and that he was not different but special what made him special would eventually define his purpose. She told him that with time his purpose would be revealed. Meanwhile, Johnny had to work at becoming the best chicken Johnny could become. Penelopy told Johnny that what others said, or thought did not define who he was unless he let it. She understood that the words were hurtful.

There was not much danger for the chicks in the chicken yard, but there was in the farmyard. That is why the chicks were not allowed to go into the farmyard. Bruster made sure that no one left the chicken yard. He told them that there was a monster out there that would swoop down from the sky and they would never be seen again. The monster was called "The Swoosh Monster". No one had seen it, but they knew it had swooshed down and chickens disappeared. Never to be seen again. All they saw was a fastmoving black spot on the ground and "swoosh" someone disappeared. Because of that, Bruster saw to it no one could leave the chicken yard.

The Adventure

Penelopy saw Johnny getting bored and she wanted to give him excitement and a variety of life experiences. She wanted Johnny to become the best bird he could be. She knew that broadening his world with new experiences and places he would grow up a wiser rooster. Penelopy knew where some chicken wire was loose in the fence that went around the chicken yard. There was just enough room for Penelopy and Johnny to squeeze through. On several occasions when no one was looking, Penelopy took Johnny down to the pond. Johnny loved the pond adventures. Life around the pond was completely different, different bugs, different vegetation, and different seeds.

The Swoosh monster strikes again

One day when Penelopy and Johnny were taking a cool splash in the pond, Penelopy did not see the chicken hawk circling above them circling around. His name was Charlie the Chicken Hawk. He was one of the things Bruster always watched out for in the chicken yard. Chicken hawks love to eat baby chickens! Johnny was looking tasty to Charlie. Little did they know He was the swoosh monster. Charlie circled around one more time and with the greatest of speed and accuracy Charlie swooped down and from out of nowhere he grabbed poor Johnny up with his talion's. With a big swish Johnny was gone! Charlie flew higher and higher with Johnny and Johnny's home got further and farther away. Johnny was wiggling with all his might trying to wiggle loose and plucking with his little beak as fast and hard as he could at the hawks' legs. He was trying to make Charlie turn him loose. When he could not break loose himself, he cried out to Farmer Charmer to save him. Although he only made loud chirps Farmer

Charmer heard him and he understood. Suddenly Charlie went splat! Charlie was trying so hard not to drop Johnny he was not watching where he was going and flew straight into the weathervane on top of the barn. Kerplunk! Johnny fell out of his talion's and rolled down the barn roof and into a pile of hay. The hay hid Johnny and Charlie could not see him anymore. He was not sure if he wanted Johnny any way, he was too much trouble. Johnny ran as fast as he could back to the chicken coop. Johnny and Penelopy both were so scared they both swore not to ever leave the safety of the chicken coop again. Never to adventure beyond the opening in the fence, never again to see the beauty beyond the chicken yard. Restricting themselves to the simple life of the chicken yard and coop. The chicken coop was at least safe. Never were they ever going to take a chance again.

Everyone on the farm was talking about the incident. They were saying that the Swish Monster was a Chicken Hawk all along. The black spot they saw was the chicken hawks shadow. They did not need to fear the shadow but see it as a warning of danger. Because they did not know what was happening, they feared it. Once they knew it was a chicken hawk, they felt better because they knew all they had to do was to keep a vigilant eye out for him and avoid him. Just knowing the truth made them feel less fearful. But everyone noticed, on the same day Johnny went for a flight with Charlie. Farmer Charmer, looking like he was going hunting, went into the woods and Charlie was never seen again. Okay so that is all for today. I would love to stay a while longer, but it is feeding time. You come back to the farm and I will tell you another tale. In the chronicles of Farmer Charmers Farm.

DISCUSSION POINTS

1. Never give up on your hopes and prayers. When you least expect it, they can be answered. That is what happened to Penelopy.

2. If you feel unattractive you can change it. Unattractive can grow into something beautiful. Can an unattractive heart be changed?

3. You may not grow out of being a bully because it is a product of your heart. A heart can be mended. Nothing beautiful ever grew out of Bulling.

4. Family is who you say is your family. Family is where your heart is. Family does not always share the same blood.

5. Being different is not a bad thing. It is your blessing. We are all different.

6. We are often afraid of what we do not understand. Seeking knowledge of it will often remove our fear of it and help prevent what we fear happening to us.

7. Playing it safe narrows our world. Is it better to take chances?

8. Who is the historian in your family? Is it important to know your family's stories?

A New Life in the Chicken Coop

After the experience with Charlie the Chicken Hawk, Johnny stayed close to Penelopy. Penelopy had been blessed again by Farmer Charmer with another chick to raise. The chicks name was Sarah, she became known as Daring Sarah Dara. She got that name riding magic sticks, but I will have to tell you about that another time. Right now, I want to continue telling you about Johnny. Penelopy loved her chicks and would not let them leave her side and they didn't want to leave her side. Sarah Dara and Johnny grew and grew until they were not little chicks. One day Johnny had a very, very strange desire. A desire he could not control. He wanted to, to, well, he wanted to crow! Johnny didn't want to crow because that meant he was a rooster. He knew he felt different and looked different, but being a rooster had its issues. He knew that only one rooster could be in the chicken pen. The farm already had a rooster and that was Bruster! Roosters crow at first ray of sunshine in the morning and wake everyone on the farm which started the day. Johnny felt this was a very responsible job and Bruster could have it. Besides the farm could only have one rooster. Another thing, roosters could fly. Not much, but they could fly to the top of the fence post or other high places. High enough that when they crowed the whole farm could hear them. Johnny could not fly, since his experience with the chicken hawk he had no desire to fly. He never wanted to fly again. He had gained a fear of heights, thanks to that roll down the barn roof.

Johnny found that he could not stop himself from wanting to crow. He didn't know what to do. One morning just at daybreak, when the sun had just started to come up. Everyone on the farm was still asleep. Johnny could not sleep, even though he tried he could not sleep. As the sun caused a crack of sun light coming over the horizon the sun beams were calling to him. He could not ignore those beams! Up he jumped on the top of the chicken coop and out it came! Churp ah de churp, oh my gosh how embarrassing. Not cocka doodle do, but churp ah de churp.

Johnny Becomes A Rooster

That day everyone on the farm was talking. Johnny's attempt at crowing was heard by everyone, even Bruster. Everyone wondered what was Ole Bruster going to do? Two roosters would never do, one had to go! Bruster was a brave rooster, and Johnny was afraid of his own shadow and would not leave his mother's side. He certainly was not made of the stuff a rooster needed to have to be a rooster in charge of a chicken pen. The rooster was an important position on the farm. If something bad wondered into the chicken yard the rooster was the one to chase it out. Sometimes the rooster had to be aggressive, Johnny didn't have an aggressive bone in his body.

Bruster was restless he certainly could not chance this little junior to grow stronger or become brave and realize his potential. Bruster knew that if Johnny learned to hold his head up high, he would learn to fly, because you can now fly with your head down. Johnny had no self esteem because of living his fear of everything beyond his mother's side.

Bruster knew he had to act quick. So, Bruster devised a plan to rid himself of Johnny. One day Bruster caught Johnny when he was in the middle of the chicken yard, and in front of everyone. First, he scared Penelopy and made her runaway. He didn't want her to help Johnny, and she was not match for Bruster. Bruster was going to fight Johnny! If Bruster won, Johnny would have to leave the farm. Johnny had nowhere safe to run to and avoid Bruster. Johnny was as scared as he was the day Charlie nabbed him, maybe even more. Johnny didn't want to fight and Penelopy had always taught him that fighting never solved anything.

The Fight

Suddenly Bruster jumped on Johnny's back and started to bite and claw with his talons. Johnny started to run as fast as he could and ran into the chicken coop. Johnny was calling for help again, to Farmer Charmer. With Bruster on his back, Bruster was high enough that when Johnny went through the opening of the coop Bruster's head hit the coop and knocked him out. Bruster laid on the ground out cold.

Luckily Farmer Charmer came out when he heard all the commotion. He knew what was going on because he had heard the churp ah de churp from Johnny and he knew that this confrontation would eventually happen. But he had already made plans to settle the matter himself. Farmer Charmer told him that because he called out to him when the chicken hawk had him, he had been watching over Johnny, even though Johnny didn't know it. Farmer Charmer knew this day would come. He took Bruster to a neighboring farm that wanted a rooster even though they didn't have chickens. They liked a rooster waking them up in the morning. There Bruster could live with no one to bully for as long as he wanted. So that's how Johnny became our rooster. You should see him now, he learned to be proud. All of that happened three summers ago and Johnny is not little anymore. He grew into his legs and feet, he filled out well, and he's not afraid anymore. He is a beautiful bird and we are proud of him as well. No one teases him about his looks anymore. Everything worked out for Johnny. The swoosh monster is gone, and everyone can take an adventure occasionally, with Johnny watching over them of course. Every morning Johnny gives a great big "Cock A Doodle Do" from the top of the barn. Yes, the barn. Johnny quickly grew out of his fear of lying.

That's all I have time to tell you about now, I'm tired of storytelling for now. Check in with me sometime and I will tell you more stories about life of the animals on Farmer Charmers farm.

Discussion

1. What options did Johnny have? Was Johnny a coward because he didn't want to fight?
2. Did Johnny have to stand his ground?
3. Was Bruster bad for wanting to fight Johnny?
4. What fears do you have and why?
5. What fear have you been confronted with? Did the confrontation cause you to overcome the fear?

Can you imagine not wanting to be who or what you are, or not wanting to look the way you look? I guess everyone does not like something about themselves. Everyone wants to change something about themselves. But what if you were a beautiful rooster and wanted to be an ugly sea gull. Johnnie had become what we call a "Wantabe".

That happened at Mr. Charmers farm. It is quite funny really. Let me tell you all about it. As you know I am Gretta the goat. I like being a goat. I am beautiful and I know it. I know it because every time someone sees me, they yell "a goat!" and then they run over to me to pet me and give me treats. So, I must be good looking. Everyone loves goats, they want our milk to make soap and cheese. How cool is that?

Well, back to the story. It all happened like this:

Johnny is now the rooster on Mr. Charmers farm, who is also known as Farmer Charmer. Johnny is a handsome rooster, he has long beautiful tail feathers of many colors and all the hens in the chicken coop swoon over him. But he did not notice that. He is kind of in charge around here, but he took that for granite.

Johnny had begun to daydream of other thangs. He knew he was a bird but a bird that could not really fly. Sure, he could manage to fly to the top of the chicken coop each morning to crow. But he wanted to really fly. He wanted to soar in the sky and surf the wind. He was also tired of scratching and pecking at the ground to peck up bugs or grain that had been thrown out by Mrs. Charmer. He wanted to spot food, soar down and pluck up his dinner. Can you believe Johnny even became ashamed of his looks? He had long scrawny legs, big feet, and a comb on his head that just flopped to one side. A comb! What was he to do with a comb? Comb his tail feathers?

Johnny even went so far as to try not to crow in the morning when the sun came up. All he knew was, Farmer Charmer acted angry every morning when he woke him up. So, he thought Farmer Charmer did not like him. One time he tried to hide his head in a pile of hay so that he would not see the sun, but it did not work. Suddenly the wind blew some of the hay away and a small beam of light broke through and he saw it. Cocka Doodle Do! He had done it again! On another morning he tried to hold his breath and keep his eyes closed tight. If he were out of breath he could not crow and if his eyes were closed, he would not see the sun. Good plan, right? Nope, it still happened. He held his breath till he started to pass out. Would not you know on his way down to the ground (because he was passing out) he opened his eyes and out came a bigger than usual Cocka Doodle Do! Johnny thought of all kinds of birds he would rather be.

One day there was a big commotion in the chicken coop. A strange looking bird sat smack dab in the middle and all the hens were squawking about him. They were all saying, "He does not belong here." "What is he?" "Who is he?" "How did he get here?" Johnny moved in for a closer look at this strange bird. The hens circled around it and said, "He was ugly?" Johnny asked "Who are you?" The intruder looked up at Johnny with a confused look and said, "I am Sandy the sea Gull, where am I?" Johnny looked at the grey and white bird in bewilderment. How long had he longed to be a sea gull? Here one was right in front of him! Sandy looked at Johnny, blinked his eyes twice and said, "You look like a rooster, although I have never seen one." Johnny stuck out his chest and stood up straight and said ", "I am a rooster and you are in my chicken coop on Mr. Charmers farm." "Why are you here?" "How did you get here and what do you want?" I don't want anything; said Sandy "I didn't mean to come here. There was a big storm on the beach. It caught me up into the clouds and blew me here. When the wind quit blowing, it dumped me here. I am all tuckered out and confused." A rooster! Sandy said. I have always wished I were a rooster. Wow look at you! You are so lucky to be a rooster!"

Johnny looked at the strange looking bird with bewilderment. How long had he longed to be a sea gull? Here was one right in front of him! "I have always wanted to be a sea gull," said Johnny. "I have always wanted to soar high above the ocean and dive down to catch a fish. What fun that would be!" "I could do that instead of scratching and pecking the ground for my food. How boring!" Sandy looked at Johnny in bewilderment, blinked twice and said: "You have it made!" "I have always wanted to be a rooster like you." "You are protected and fed by the farmer. You worry for nothing. Sorry, but I think you are ungrateful for what you have because you do not appreciate what you have.

Maybe that is because you do not understand what life is like for me. Let me tell you about the life of a seagull. Yes, I can dive for my food. If I get it, I then fight off the other seagulls to keep it. Seagulls must scavenge for food. We do not have a shelter. You have a nice place provided for you. Someone feeds you. You do not have to scavenge for food. But most importantly, just look at you! You are a beautiful bird. You have lots of color. Not gray and white like me. I think seagulls are ugly and roosters are beautiful and Johnny you are important to this farm." "Important?" asked Johnny "Yes, important "said Sandy. "You would be missed if you were gone and the hens need you. You are blessed to live here and be you."

"Wow!" said Johnny. "I never realized how lucky I was."

"Well, the storm is long gone, and I need to get back to the ocean" said Sandy. "You can stay here." Said Johnny "Oh no," said Sandy "that would be like a fish out of water, I need to get back to the ocean. But there is one thing I want before I go." "What's that?" said Johnny. "Would you give me one big Cocka Doodle Do before I go?" Johnny stuck his chest out big, leaned his head real far back and with a big flap of his wings he belted out the biggest Cocka doodle do the farm had ever hear. Must say, it confused everyone that did not know what was going on. But after that, Sandy said goodbye to everyone and flew off never to be seen again.

"Imagine that" said Johnny "What I wanted to be, wanted to be me."

Discussion Points

1. Is it O.K. to daydream about being something else? Wouldn't that be how we decide what we want to be in life?
2. Did Johnny not appreciate all he had or who he was?
3. There will always be storms in life that gets us off tract, but we can always get back on track.
4. Is it possible for someone you want to be like, want to be like you?
5. Do you know what self-esteem is?
6. Do you think Johnny loved himself?

I'm sorry, that is all the stories I can tell you for now. I would love to tell you more in the future. There is a lot to tell to chronical the life and adventures of everyone on Farmer Charmers Farm. Who doesn't love farm animals? It only takes a few months for a baby farm animal to grow into maturity. But a lot can happen in that time. There are many more stories about the animals on Farmer Charmers Farm. I wanted to tell you about the magic sticks and the pumpkin explosion but I will have to save those stories for another time. Bye Bye for now!

The End

Lightning Source UK Ltd.
Milton Keynes UK
UKHW051334140620
364900UK00007B/343